Panzee Plays Hide-and-Seek

It was a beautiful day on ZingZilla Island.

The ZingZillas were in the Glade with DJ Loose listening to tubular bells.

The tubular bells made dinging, donging, ringing, singing noises and they were very **LOUD**.

Panzee shouted, "Let's write a song about bells!"

"With a ding dong, ding dong,
ding dong, ding dong, ding dong,
ding dong - ringing on a bell,"

the ZingZillas sang.
Soon the bell song was finished.

"Let's play hide-and-seek!" said Zak.

"**Yay!!!**" Drum cheered.

"I'm no good at hide-and-seek," said Panzee.

"Don't worry," said Tang.
"We'll do the hiding and you do the seeking. **That's the fun bit!**"

But Panzee wasn't sure.

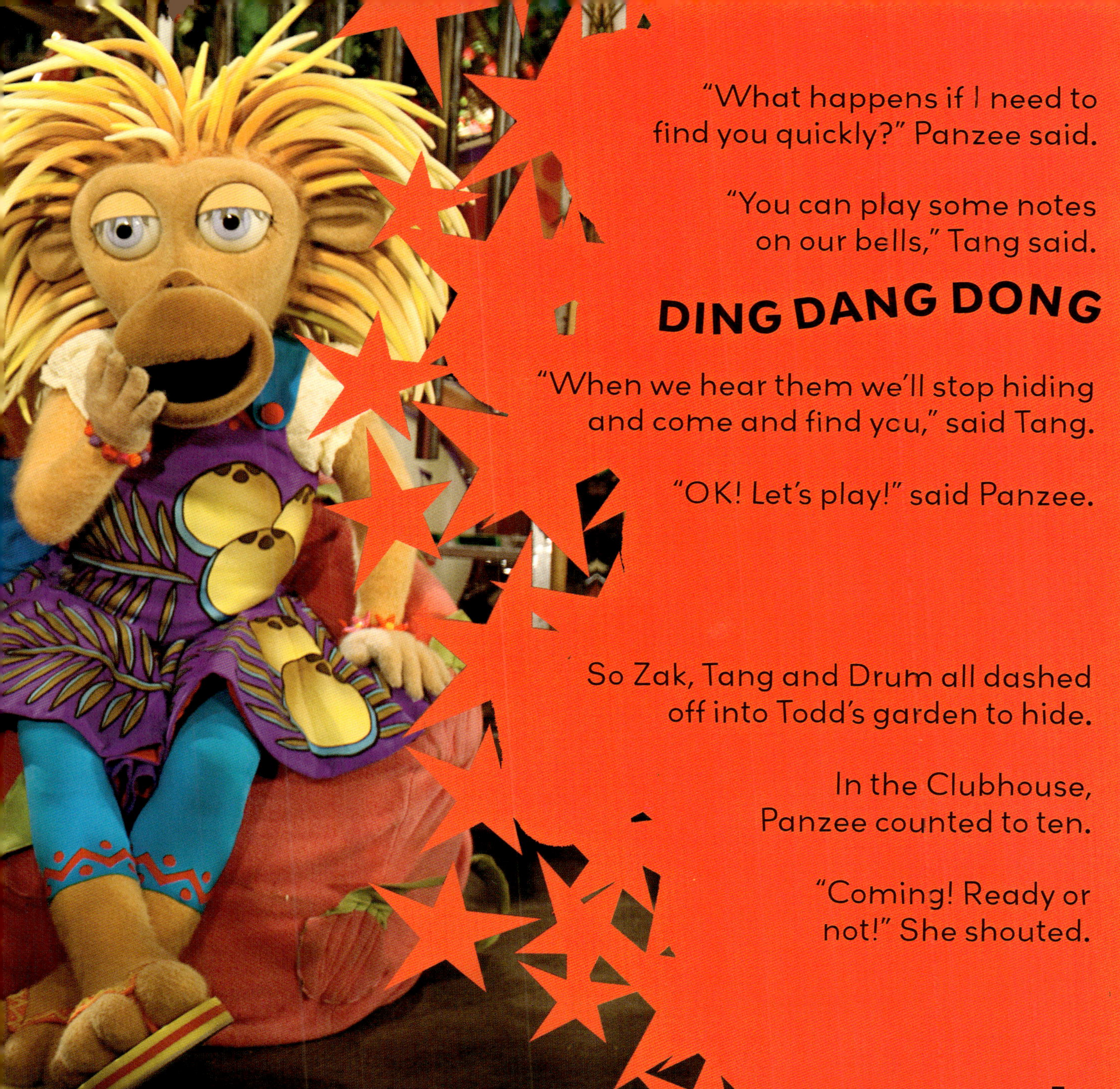

"What happens if I need to find you quickly?" Panzee said.

"You can play some notes on our bells," Tang said.

DING DANG DONG

"When we hear them we'll stop hiding and come and find you," said Tang.

"OK! Let's play!" said Panzee.

So Zak, Tang and Drum all dashed off into Todd's garden to hide.

In the Clubhouse, Panzee counted to ten.

"Coming! Ready or not!" She shouted.

Panzee started to look carefully for the others but she couldn't find them.

"This is really hard," she thought to herself.

Panzee walked over to the bells. "If I just played the notes, then I'd find the others really quickly!"

So Panzee played the notes:

DING DANG DONG.

Down in Todd's garden, Tang heard the sound of the bells. So Tang, Drum and Zak rushed back to the Clubhouse.

"There! I've found you!" Panzee laughed.

"**But that's not fair!**" said Zak. "We only came back because we heard you play the bells!"
"Let's play again," said Tang. "Only this time you must look for us properly."

"OK," sighed Panzee.

This time Tang, Drum and Zak hid in the Coconut Hut.

Tang and Drum hid behind the counter, while Zak hid under a tablecloth.

But in the Clubhouse, Panzee wasn't happy.

"Hide-and -seek is really hard and it takes forever," she said. "If I play the notes on the bells again, then everyone will come back and we can play a different game."

So Panzee played the notes...

DING DANG DONG.

"That's Panzee again!" said Zak. "She must really need us!"

Zak, Tang and Drum rushed back to the Clubhouse.

"I found you!" Panzee smiled. "Now we can play a new game. I hope you don't mind."

"**We do mind!**" said the others.

Tang was cross. "Panzee, you must play the game properly. Let's try one more time."

"OK," nodded Panzee sadly.

Panzee counted to 10. But suddenly she had a big thought. It was almost time for the Big Zing!

“I need to tell the others quickly! I know! I’ll play the bells. That will bring them back.”

DING DANG DONG.

But Zak, Tang and Drum heard the notes and decided to stay hidden.

“That’s Panzee again!” said Tang. “She’s not going to trick us this time!”

Panzee dinged and donged and danged, but none of her dinging, donging and danging was working! "Oh no!" she said. "This is a disaster!"

"You shouldn't have tricked your friends, Panzee." DJ Loose said as he appeared at the Clubhouse door.

"But it's almost time for the Big Zing, DJ!" Panzee said. "What am I going to do?"

Panzee gazed at the bells sadly. And then she had another idea!

Panzee and DJ dashed back to the Glade. They played the tubular bells really, really **LOUD!!**

The sound of the tubular bells made everything in the jungle **SHAAAAAAAKE.**

It made Zak, Tang and Drum shake too!

"Where is that loud sound coming from?!" shouted Zak.

"Let's go and find out!" called Tang.

Zak, Drum and Tang found Panzee back in the Clubhouse.

"I'm really sorry I tricked you before," she said.

"That's alright," said Zak. "Thank you for saying sorry."

"So why did you need us
so quickly?" asked Tang.
"Because..." said Panzee,

"It's Big Zing Time!"

And so, when the last coconut had fallen and the Moaning Stones had whizzed round the island, DJ Loose said,

"It's that time of the day when we like to say:
It's Big Zing Time! So take it away!"

And the ZingZillas sang their **Dinging Donging Bell Song.**

Afterwards, everyone agreed:

That was the best Big Zing EVER